Mac at Camp

Mac is a fun puppy.
He goes camping
with the Franklins.
They set up camp
by the lake.

Mac likes to camp.
He likes to chase the loons
on the lake.
The loons quack and swim.
They fly away from Mac.

Mac likes to hunt
in the moonlight.
While hunting,
Mac finds raccoons.
There is a mother
and a baby.

Mac zooms over
to the little raccoons.
The mother raccoon shows
Mac some teeth.
She hisses and rages
at him twice.

Mac is not foolish.
He hides behind a hedge.
Soon Mac runs back
to camp.
He sleeps for a while.
Then he wakens.

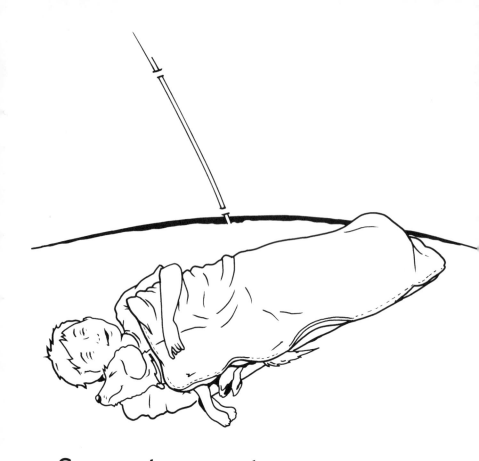

Something is hooting
up in a tree.
The tree is right next to Mac.
The pup gets spooked.
He gets into the tent
with Sam.
Now he feels safe!

Mac and the Glue

Mac, the pup, is the only one at home.
It is wet and stormy outside. He must stay in the kitchen until Mom gets back.

Mac finds a tube
of white glue in the kitchen.
He pokes it with his nose.
He holds it in his teeth.
Oops!
Mac bit a hole in the tube.

The white glue leaks.
The glue sticks
to the blue rug.
It sticks to the boots
on the rug.
The glue sticks
to the broom handle.

It sticks to Mac's dog food...
...and it sticks to Mac's tooth.
Soon Mac can't unlock
his teeth.
They are stuck together.

They will not budge!
What a sticky mess
for foolish Mac!

Soon Mom comes home
to rescue the silly pup.
She is not mad.
Mac is lucky that Mom is
so nice.

Sam's Book

It is nearly bedtime.
Sam pulls a book
off the shelf.
The book has a thick,
black spine.
The spine has gold print.

Sam pulls a pillow
from his bed.
He grabs his blanket, too.
He takes everything
to the reading nook.

The reading nook is
a window seat.
It is the best place to read.
Sam sits under his blanket
and begins his story.

Mom and Dad will read
their books, too.
Mom pops a bowl
of popcorn.
Dad puts a bundle of wood
on the fire.

Mom reads a cookbook.
She dreams about cooking
a splendid meal.
Dad reads a fishing book.
He dreams of hooking
a huge salmon.

Sam is deep into
his fantastic story.
He is not in the window seat.
He is not in the book nook.
Sam is not even at home.
He has gone away
to a distant place.

Sam has gone
on an amazing trip.
He is the hero in a fantastic
rocket ship.
Then the book ends
and Sam is back
in the reading nook.

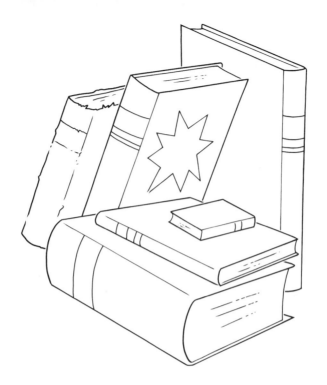

Books

Thin books, thick books, tall books, small books. Black books, blue books, old books, new books.

Books that make you mad
or sad.
Books you like to read with Dad.
Books that make you shake
with fright.
(That kind shouldn't be read
at night.)

Books by Dr. Seuss.
Books by Mother Goose.
Books with Jack and Jill.
They went up a hill.

Cookbooks, songbooks,
fairy tales, scary tales.
Books with puzzles, books
with riddles,
books with secrets
in their middles.

Try *Make Way for Ducklings*,
would you?
Get *Snowy Day*,
could you?

Read of rabbits that live
in the wood.
Read of Snow White
or Robin Hood.

Grab a book from a shelf.
Read the book by yourself.
Take your blanket to a nook.
Sit and read a grand
good book.

A Monsoon Soon!

This is your fishy news program.
We have some important news for the fish in the pond.
In a little while, there is going to be a monsoon!

A monsoon is a bad storm.
The wind zooms fast
and the rain is thick.
You can't feel the wind deep
in the water, but there will be
strong waves.

Deep puddles will form
on the sand.
The water might get cold.
It will seem very dark.
Branches and telephone
cables might get blown
into the pond.

Don't do anything foolish.
For the next few days,
stay near your fish castle.
Wiggle your fins and swim
to the bottom of the pond.
You will be safe deep
underneath the storm.

Party in Jig's Yard

Jig and Nip will have
a party soon.
They will sing their songs
and play a tune.

They'll have the party
at the farm
with music in Jig's pen
and food in the barn.

Whether you are near or far,
take a bus or drive a car,
run or jog or fly or hop,
race to the party!
Quick! Don't stop!

To find Jig's pen won't be hard.
Follow the moonlight
to his yard.
The party is where the bright
lights are.
Just a few quick steps
and it's under a star!

Come in, Mr. Raccoon.
Come in, Miss Loon.
Come in Mrs. Finch.
Come sing a tune.

We'll wiggle and giggle
and then we'll dance.
We'll sing and clap
and chuckle and prance.

Stories by Susan Ebbers (Mac at Camp, Mac and the Glue,
Sam's Book, Books) and Sue Jones (A Monsoon Soon!,
Party in Jig's Yard)
Illustrations by Deborah Wolfe Ltd.

Volume 26, ISBN: 1-931728-27-5

ISBN 1-931728-27-5

PhonicsWorks™ Reader

15

Table of Contents